ISABELLA PAGLIA is an Italian author who has written over a dozen children's books. Her titles have received multiple awards across Italy, including the Pippi Prize and the "Giacomo Giulitto" National Prize for Children's Literature. *The Box* is Isabella's English-language debut. Visit her website at isabellapaglia.info.

PAOLO PROIETTI is the illustrator of *Before We Sleep* and *The Friendship Surprise* (both Red Comet Press). Often inspired by Studio Ghibli films, Paolo works in chalk, pastel, and watercolor paint to create his illustrations. He lives in Italy. Follow Paolo on Instagram @pallo_illustrations.

LAURA WATKINSON translates books for children and adults from Italian, German, and Dutch. Her translations have received numerous honors, including three Mildred L. Batchelder Awards and the Vondel Translation Prize. Laura lives in the Netherlands. Visit her website at laurawatkinson.com.

To every child's smile.
They are our sunshine and make our hearts
take wing.

— I. P.

To my Scimmione, Pallo, Lara, Amelie,
and Totoro . . . my family.

— P. P.

First published in the United States in 2022 by Eerdmans Books for Young Readers,
an imprint of Wm. B. Eerdmans Publishing Co., Grand Rapids, Michigan
www.eerdmans.com/youngreaders

Text © 2020 Isabella Paglia • Illustrations © 2020 Paolo Proietti
Originally published in Italy as *La Scatola* • © 2020 la Margherita edizioni, via Milano 73/75, 20010 Cornaredo (Milan), Italy

This edition published by arrangement with Books Everywhere Agency • English-language translation © Laura Watkinson 2022

30 29 28 27 26 25 24 23 22   1 2 3 4 5 6 7 8 9

ISBN 978-0-8028-5592-3 • A catalog record of this book is available from the Library of Congress

Illustrations created with pastel, chalk, and watercolor paint

The Box

written by
Isabella Paglia

illustrated by
Paolo Proietti

translated by **Laura Watkinson**

EERDMANS BOOKS FOR YOUNG READERS

GRAND RAPIDS, MICHIGAN

What was that box doing
there in the middle of the forest?
It was a mystery. One morning,
the animals woke up and . . .

surprise!

There was a strange box
with two holes in the side!

Big enough for someone or something
to fit inside. Big enough to hide in.

"Hmm . . . a box with eyes?"

"How did it get here?"

"When did it arrive?"

"Who could have brought it into the forest?" the curious animals wondered.

"Hey, I think there's someone inside . . ."

The box started to shake.
Everyone jumped.
Yes, there really was
someone in there!

"Welcome to the forest!" the animals shouted,
so that whoever was inside the box could hear them.
But the box was silent and did not move.

"Come on! Come on out!"

"It's springtime. The sun's shining and making us
nice and warm. There's no need for you to stay
hidden away in the dark."

oooOOOI!"

The box gave a cry. The voice
creaked and croaked, as if whoever
was in there had a really dry throat.
But it clearly said NO.

The animals took a step back.

"They don't want to come out. But why not?"

"Maybe they feel ugly or different or like they don't belong," said Bear.

"Or they could be having a rough day. One of those days when you don't like anything or anyone, and you feel really sad, and nothing seems right!" suggested Squirrel.

"Something bad might have happened to them out here, and now they're scared," Fox said.

"Perhaps they came out and met someone who was mean and greedy with big, sharp claws, so they decided they'd rather stay inside the box!" Hare squeaked.

"Well, if that's true, we could be frightening them . . ." Owl said.

And they all took another step back.

"Why don't we do something fun to entertain them?"

"We can tell jokes and do somersaults and pretend to be clowns. Like at the circus!"

"Yes, let's put on a show!"

Dressed in costumes and full of goodwill, the animals put on the greatest show the forest had ever seen, with music and performances and bright, shiny colors.

But . . .

. . . nothing happened!

The sun was setting on the horizon.
The box was still firmly closed.

"All right. Let's try again tomorrow,"
the animals said, still not losing hope.

The next morning, the animals had a meeting.

"What we need is another idea . . . "

"How about a party?"

"Yes, with lots of decorations and delicious
cakes and cookies and lemonade!"

"Maybe this time the box will decide to open up."

So that was what they did.

The box began to rumble away
like a hungry little tummy . . .

But . . . nothing.

The box stayed shut!

"Never mind! We'll try again tomorrow. Don't lose heart!"

The next morning, clouds filled the sky.
Before anyone else was around, Bear snuck up
to the box and gave it a cuddle.

A few minutes later, Fox came along and wrapped
her tail around the box in a gentle hug.

While no one was looking, Squirrel popped a few
nuts through the two holes in the side.

Hare arranged fresh daisies all around the box.

Owl placed a broken blade of grass on top
of it, next to a long, unbroken blade.

The little eyes inside the box came closer
to the holes.

But then, above the forest,
a flash of lightning streaked across the sky,
followed by a terrible rumble of thunder.

The rain came pouring down.

The animals knew they had to
do something—and fast!

"Quickly! Our friend needs somewhere
to shelter. Or they'll get soaked!"

Running, the animals
carried the box into Bear's den,
where it was warm and snug.

"Are you okay in there, little friend?"

The box shook with a fluttering of wings, and then . . . it opened right up!

"Thank you so much, everyone, for waiting for me," said the creature with a squawk.

"We don't know what happened to you, but we do know that even a little blade of grass can bend and break if it's battered by the wind and rain," said Owl. "Maybe all you needed to help you open up was some friends . . . *us!*"